The Big Bang Book

Toys and Games to Make

David Pitt

GRANADA

Contents

Introduction

4

The projects in this book are suitable for children of about 8 years old and above. However, some of them involve cutting with craft knives and scissors, and using glue. Also, some of the materials need to be handled carefully – things like kebab skewers with sharp points and the edges of metal foil. So please be careful.

Big Bang is a Granada Media Children's Production

First published in Great Britain in 2001

by Granada Media an imprint of Andre Deutsch Limited
20 Mortimer Street
London W1V 5HA

In association with Granada Media Group

Text and photographs copyright © Granada Media Group Ltd 2001

The right of David Pitt to be identified as the author of this work has been asserted by him in accordance with the Copyright, Designs and Patents Act 1988.

A catalogue record for this book is available from the British Library.

ISBN: 0 233 99949 3

Editor: Nicky Paris
Photography: Andy Snaith
Design: Russell Porter, Jon Lucas, Sarah Williams
Production: Alastair Gourlay

Printed and bound in Italy by Eurolitho

10 9 8 7 6 5 4 3 2 1

1 Toys and Games

Introduction

Welcome to The Big Bang Book!
All the projects are designed to look nice when they're made, as well as being fun things to have and play with. We hope you have as much fun making them as we did. Before you start, here are a few tips. Happy constructing!

Read through the instructions COMPLETELY before starting. That way you will have a sense of how the finished project should look and work and whether you'll need an older person to help you.

The items range in difficulty from pretty easy (one 'pair of scissors'), which should take no more than 15 minutes to make; to quite tricky (five 'pairs of scissors'), which you should only attempt if you've got a degree in advanced gluing. Seriously, the harder projects are all possible, but you should expect them to be fiddly, and to take a few days (with a bit of rest and relaxation in the middle).

The projects are designed to be made from stuff you'll find lying around in your house. We are big fans of:

a) the stiff cardboard tubes you get in the middle of rolls of foil and cling film,
b) bendy drinking straws,
c) the kind of cardboard boxes that supermarkets get their fruit in,

d) wooden kebab skewers,

e) poster tubes,

f) rubber bands.

If you don't already have the right stuff,
you can buy everything from either supermarkets or stationery stores! Some of the things you'll need can be dangerous if you're not careful – like the sharp end of a kebab skewer. So always take care, and if you're in any doubt, get someone older to help.

You hardly need any tools, just a pair of scissors
and a craft knife for cutting (and if you're young, get some help with cutting!). You will need some glue for sticking stuff together – we normally use a glue gun. You can

buy 'cool melt' glue guns that are quite safe to use; or you can use ordinary PVA glue, but you'll need to leave it longer to set. We also use sticky tape – the coloured sort that you use for insulating electrical wiring is great.

Don't worry about following the instructions exactly – you may well think up better ways to achieve a good result. If you haven't got the right bits and pieces, try and think of good substitutes – for instance, you could use bits of garden cane instead of kebab skewers. Be creative, and above all – **have FUN!**

CHAPTER ONE

Toys and Games

Periscope Puppets

These puppets are great because you can see the audience while you're operating them!

You'll need:

material to dress your puppet

sticky tape

2 one-litre milk or juice cartons

kebab skewers

fishing line

You'll also need to find:
thin card, thick strong card,
plastic mirror card (you can get it in craft shops)

1. Drink the milk (or juice) and wash out the cartons. Open out the top flaps and cut off the flaps with the spouts. Cut a square hole in the side of each carton, at the bottom.

2. Now tape the two cartons together, so that the holes are at the top and bottom, and face in opposite directions.

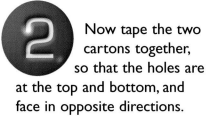

Now make the mirror supports. Take a strip of strong card, the same width as the inside of the cartons. It needs to fold to support the mirror at a 45° angle, so it's important to get the length right. Measure it in three bits: the first and second bits are the same size as the hole in the carton. The third bit needs to be just long enough to reach from corner to corner when the whole thing is folded into a right-angled triangle shape.

4 Cut a piece of mirror card so it's the same shape and size as the large bit of the support and glue it in position. Now do exactly the same again to make another mirror assembly.

5 Glue the two mirror assemblies into the two holes in the cartons so that the mirrors face you as you look into the holes. And now you've got a working periscope!

To make the periscope into a puppet cut out a mask shape for the head, with holes for the eyes. Then put a pupil in each eye which is just a small circle of cardboard, supported by a thin length of fishing line glued top and bottom. With the mask in position, you can easily see past the pupil but the audience won't notice the mirror behind…

You can decorate your periscope puppet however takes your fancy… You can make arms from kebab skewers with bits of card for hands. You can dress your puppet in bits of cloth or old pieces of material.

A periscope puppet show is great, because even though you're hiding behind the sofa, you can see exactly what the audience is doing – and make the puppets respond!

Battling Robots

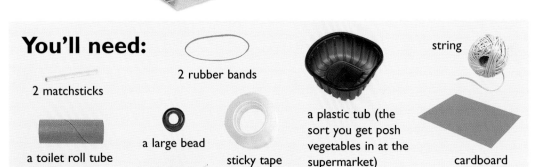

You'll need:

2 matchsticks

2 rubber bands

a toilet roll tube

a large bead

sticky tape

a plastic tub (the sort you get posh vegetables in at the supermarket)

string

cardboard

Have 'robot wars' in your bedroom with these battling 'bots...

1 Start by cutting out a disc of card about 6cm in diameter. Make two holes in the disc, one on each side of the centre. Snip a rubber band (to make one long piece of rubber), thread it through the holes and tie it at the back. Then make a second disc exactly the same!

2 The discs are the two drive wheels for your 'bot, so glue them to either end of a cardboard toilet roll tube. Then cut a length of string, tape one end to the centre of the toilet roll tube and wind the string on. This will be the robot's motor.

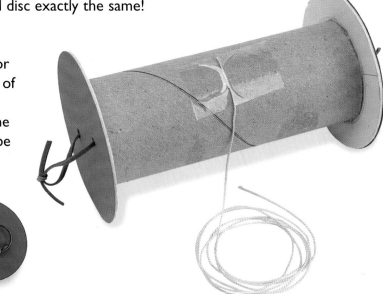

Now for the robot's body which you make from the plastic tub. The larger ones are exactly the right size for a toilet roll tube motor – which is handy! Cut small slots in both sides and a small hole in the back.

4 Now mount the motor, by stretching the rubber bands into the slots and securing them with matchsticks. Thread the end of the string out through the hole in the back.

And now you can test the robot. Pull the string, which will make the toilet roll tube turn and will wind up the rubber bands, storing the energy. When you let go, the bands unwind, spinning the motor, and driving the robot forward… or backward if you've got the motor the wrong way round. If so, just take the string off and wind it the other way.

Now tie a large bead to the end of the string. It looks neat, gives you something to pull, and most importantly stops the string disappearing into the robot every time you pull it!

7 Now the fun bit – decorating your robot. Use your imagination here – you can buy silver card in art shops that looks great when you cut out shapes and stick them on the 'bot.

holes and cut edges make it more dramatic

plastic bottle tops

drinking straws

two pieces of silver card stuck back to back

lolly stick covered in metallic sticky tape

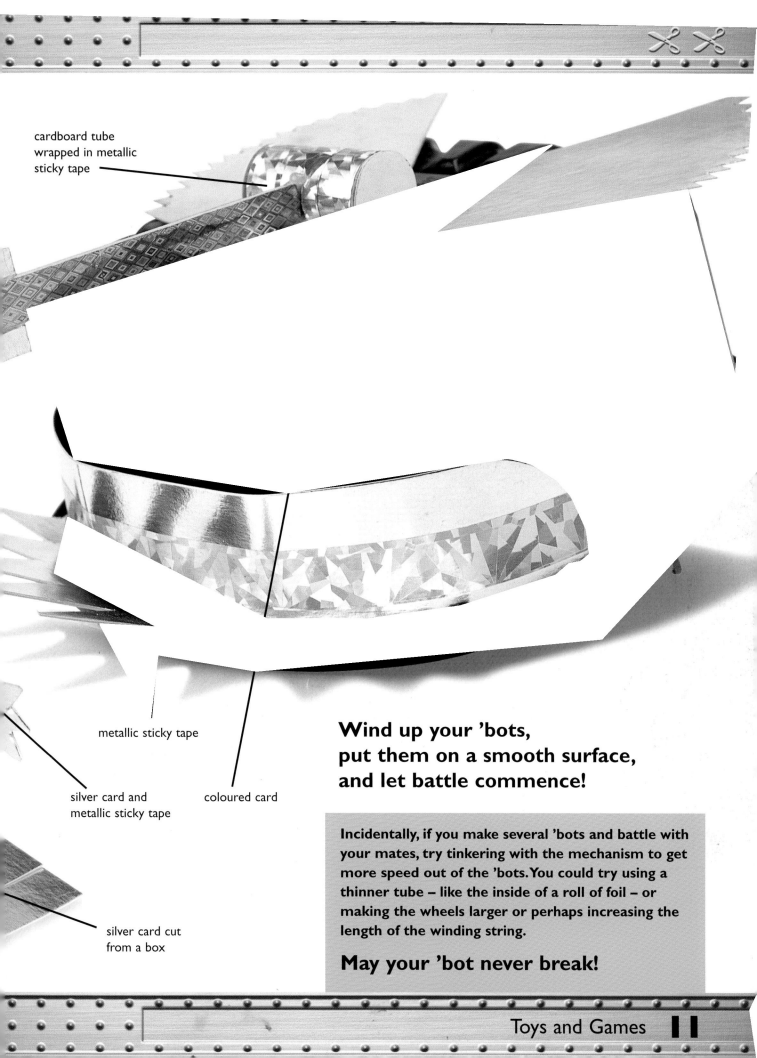

cardboard tube
wrapped in metallic
sticky tape

metallic sticky tape

coloured card

silver card and
metallic sticky tape

silver card cut
from a box

**Wind up your 'bots,
put them on a smooth surface,
and let battle commence!**

Incidentally, if you make several 'bots and battle with
your mates, try tinkering with the mechanism to get
more speed out of the 'bots. You could try using a
thinner tube – like the inside of a roll of foil – or
making the wheels larger or perhaps increasing the
length of the winding string.

May your 'bot never break!

The Amazing Unicycling Skeleton

Roll up! Roll up! Come and see the amazing scarifying skeleton as he performs daredevil and death defying feats on the high wire! Or even better – make your own…

You'll need:

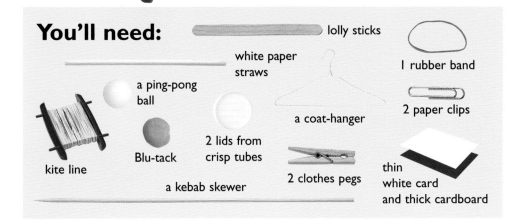

- lolly sticks
- white paper straws
- a ping-pong ball
- kite line
- Blu-tack
- 2 lids from crisp tubes
- a coat-hanger
- a kebab skewer
- 2 clothes pegs
- 1 rubber band
- 2 paper clips
- thin white card and thick cardboard

1. Begin by munching your way through two tubes of crisps. Why? Because you need the lids, silly.

2. Cut out a disc of thick card, slightly smaller than the lids. Then get some help to make a hole through the centres of the lids and the card. Thread the lids and the card disc on to a kebab skewer, with the card in the middle, and the rims of the lids pointing outwards. (The idea is that you should end up with a groove between the two lids for the high wire to fit in.) Glue the lot together, and let it dry completely. Then stretch a rubber band around the cardboard disc. This will help the unicycle grip the high wire.

3. Cut off the ends of the kebab skewer to leave about 4cm protruding on each side. Tape on some bent paper clips to make pedals.

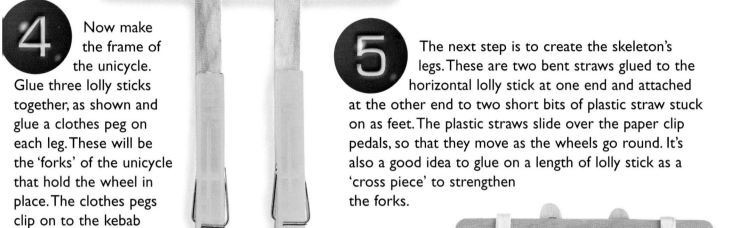

4 Now make the frame of the unicycle. Glue three lolly sticks together, as shown and glue a clothes peg on each leg. These will be the 'forks' of the unicycle that hold the wheel in place. The clothes pegs clip on to the kebab skewer, on either side of the wheel.

5 The next step is to create the skeleton's legs. These are two bent straws glued to the horizontal lolly stick at one end and attached at the other end to two short bits of plastic straw stuck on as feet. The plastic straws slide over the paper clip pedals, so that they move as the wheels go round. It's also a good idea to glue on a length of lolly stick as a 'cross piece' to strengthen the forks.

6 Next make a 'balancing arm' which will help the unicycle stay upright. Get someone who's good at cutting wire to snip the middle of the wire coat-hanger, and straighten out the two ends. Also get them to straighten out the hook. Be careful handling the coat-hanger, as the points will be very sharp!

7 Glue the opened out coat-hanger to the horizontal lolly stick on your fork assembly, so that an equal amount of wire extends on both sides, and the straightened out hook points upwards. This joint needs to be very strong, so it's a good idea to re-inforce it with lots of glue, and another lolly stick.

8 Now create the rest of the skeleton. Its backbone is a white straw, just slipped over the upright bit of wire. Then glue a ping-pong ball at the top for the skull, and cut a jaw shape and an eye socket shape from thin card and glue them in place.

9 The ribcage is made from straws bent around the spine, and the hips are thin card shapes. Copy the shapes in the picture on to a piece of white card, cut them out and glue them in place. The arms are bent straws reaching down to the coat-hanger and attached with bent paper clips.

10 To balance your skeleton so he stays upright on the unicycle, you'll need to add counter-weights to the ends of the coat-hanger. The counterweights are blobs of Blu-tack, wodged on to the wire. You'll have to experiment with different amounts until the unicycle balances properly.

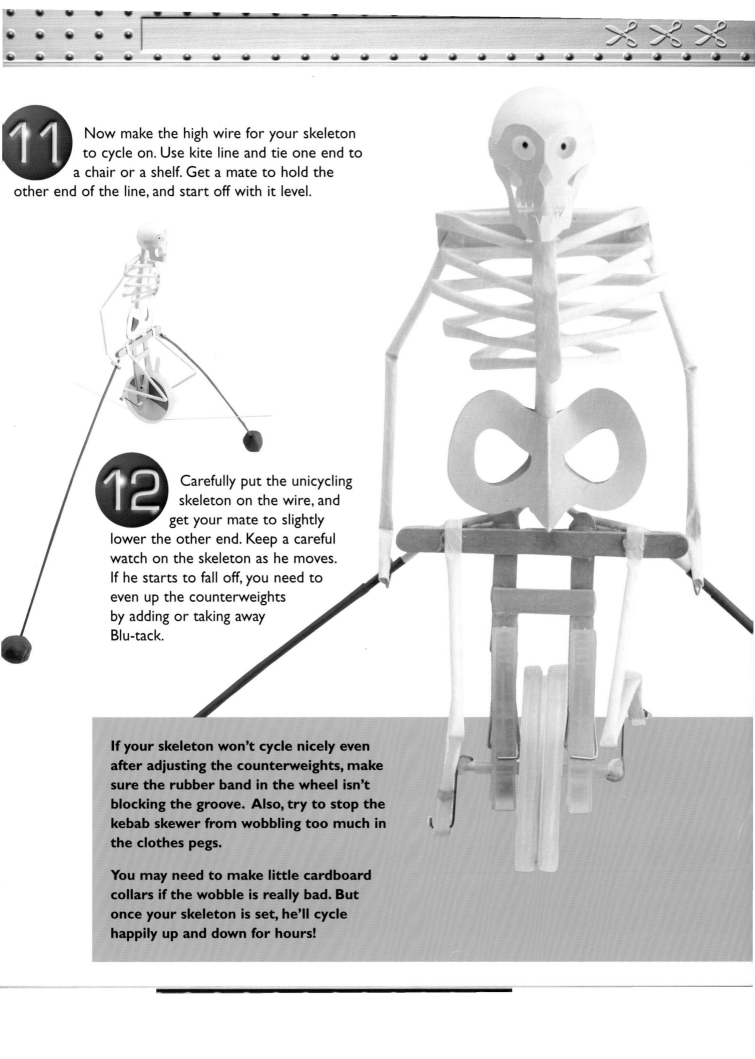

11 Now make the high wire for your skeleton to cycle on. Use kite line and tie one end to a chair or a shelf. Get a mate to hold the other end of the line, and start off with it level.

12 Carefully put the unicycling skeleton on the wire, and get your mate to slightly lower the other end. Keep a careful watch on the skeleton as he moves. If he starts to fall off, you need to even up the counterweights by adding or taking away Blu-tack.

If your skeleton won't cycle nicely even after adjusting the counterweights, make sure the rubber band in the wheel isn't blocking the groove. Also, try to stop the kebab skewer from wobbling too much in the clothes pegs.

You may need to make little cardboard collars if the wobble is really bad. But once your skeleton is set, he'll cycle happily up and down for hours!

Strange Alien Abduction Game

You'll need:

2 large vegetable or fruit boxes

8 drinking straws (the sort with a bendy bit at the top)

fishing line

green card

4 poster tubes

You'll also need to find:
some green paint, sticky tape

This game is quite hard to play, but you get a great sense of achievement when you finally manage to abduct a cow! The aim is to use the control lines to guide your flying saucer to hover over a cow, then pick it up and deliver it safely to the Mothership for... experimentation!

1 Start by making the base from two vegetable or fruit boxes. These kind of boxes are made from quite thick cardboard, so they're strong and firm, which is important. Cut off the corners that stick up, and turn the boxes upside down. Glue the two together to make your base and let the glue set.

2 Next you need to put four towers at the corners of the base. These are made from lengths of poster tube. Cut round holes in the four corners to take the tubes, and glue them FIRMLY in place. Cover the base with a piece of green card to make a grassy field and paint the towers to match.

3 Now get eight drinking straws with bendy tops. Cut off the ends to leave about 2cm on either side of the bend. These are going to be the 'guides' for your flying saucer control lines.

4 Tape two guides to each poster tube, one at the top and one at the bottom, so that the bendy bits point in towards the centre of the grassy field.

The two control lines are made from fishing line. Here's how to thread the first line (following the red lines on the diagram below):

❶ feed the first line through the bottom guide on one of the towers;
❷ run the line up the tower;
❸ feed it through the guide at the top;
❹ run the line across to the diagonally opposite tower;
❺ feed it through the top guide;
❻ run it down the tower;
❼ feed it out through the bottom guide;
❽ pass it around the outside of the tower in front and back to where you started.

After step 8 cut the line, leaving plenty of spare. Then repeat the process for the second line and the other two towers (following the blue lines).

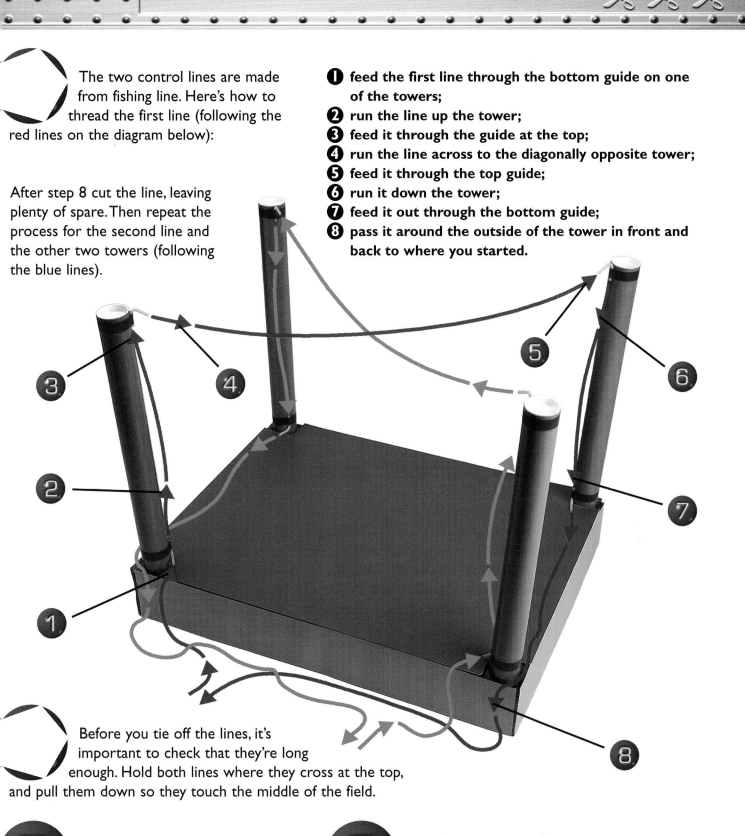

Before you tie off the lines, it's important to check that they're long enough. Hold both lines where they cross at the top, and pull them down so they touch the middle of the field.

7 You need to tie the two ends of each line together, round the outside of the base, as in the diagram, making sure that you leave plenty of slack.

8 Now if you pull the lines taut, you'll find that they cross in the middle of the four towers. This is where you'll fix the flying saucer later, but for now, just use a dab of glue to stick the lines together.

The next step is to create the flying saucer.

You'll need:

Blu-tack

a small foil pie container

a bead

a paper clip

9 The flying saucer is just one of those little foil pie containers – like the ones you get mince pies in at Christmas! Put a lump of Blu-tack in it for ballast, then turn it over. To make the hook, straighten out a paper clip, and stick it through the bottom of the foil container, so it sticks through the Blu-tack and comes out the other side. Bend the underneath bit of the paper clip into a hook.

10 Stick a bead on the top end of the paper clip hook (for decoration and safety).

11 And that's your flying saucer finished! Now fix it to the control wires where they cross, using the protruding bit of the paper clip. If you've got enough Blu-tack in the saucer, when you let go it should pull the lines through the guides. If this doesn't happen, add Blu-tack until it does!

The final step is to create the Mothership and the animals to abduct.

You'll need:

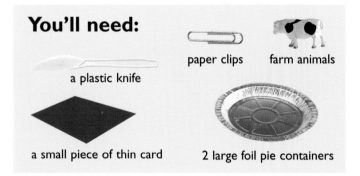

a plastic knife

paper clips

farm animals

a small piece of thin card

2 large foil pie containers

12 The Mothership is just made from the two large foil pie containers, glued together to make a large flying saucer shape. Glue a plastic knife to the bottom as shown – the reason will become clear later…

13 Cut a largish hole in the top of the Mothership, and line it with a cylinder of thin card. This is the loading bay where the farmyard animals will be delivered. Decorate the Mothership with coloured card and beads.

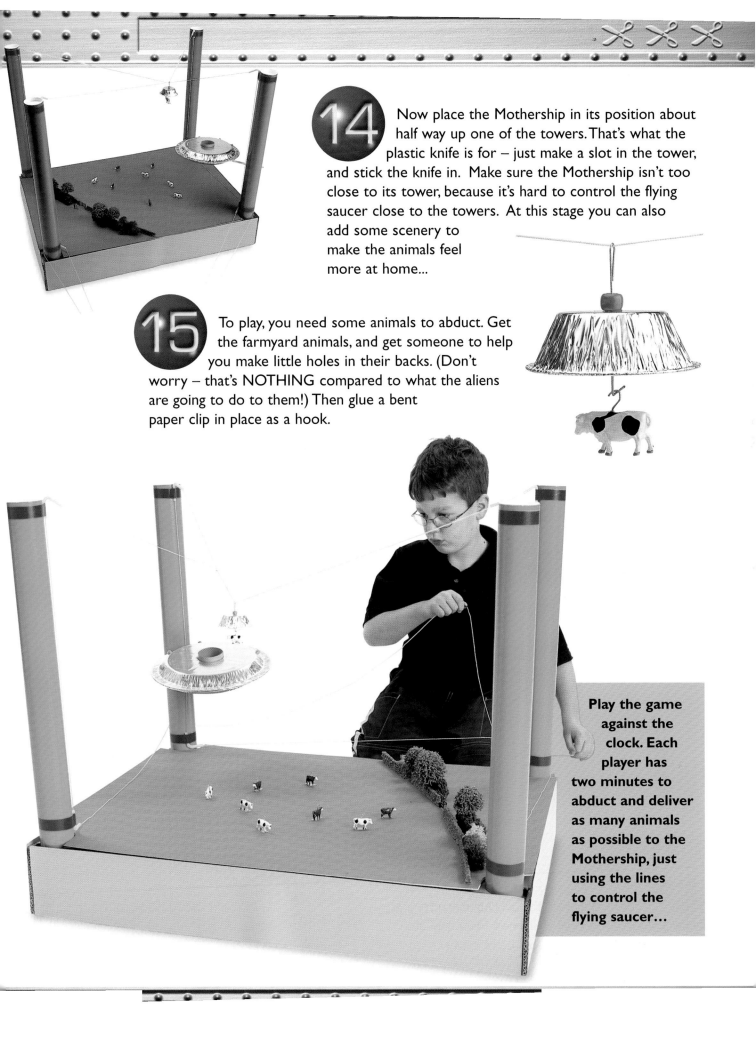

14 Now place the Mothership in its position about half way up one of the towers. That's what the plastic knife is for – just make a slot in the tower, and stick the knife in. Make sure the Mothership isn't too close to its tower, because it's hard to control the flying saucer close to the towers. At this stage you can also add some scenery to make the animals feel more at home...

15 To play, you need some animals to abduct. Get the farmyard animals, and get someone to help you make little holes in their backs. (Don't worry – that's NOTHING compared to what the aliens are going to do to them!) Then glue a bent paper clip in place as a hook.

Play the game against the clock. Each player has two minutes to abduct and deliver as many animals as possible to the Mothership, just using the lines to control the flying saucer...

Tiddlywink Battleships

The aim of this game is to sink enemy ships, by hitting them with tiddlywink missiles.

You'll need:

waterproof glue

tiddlywinks

I foil tray for each ship

a hole punch

You'll also need to find: cocktail sticks, a large water container (a plastic toy-tidy box works well)

1 To make the ships, cut out a ship shape from the base of a foil tray. Then cut little slits all around the edge.

2 Punch four holes in the bottom. Then fold up the flaps.

3 Next cut two side pieces from the left over bit of the foil tray. Each should be slightly longer than one side of the boat.

4 Glue them to the flaps of the base, using waterproof glue, and glue down the overlapping bits at the front and back.

For the cabins, cut out rectangular bits of foil tray, and bend them into 'U' shapes. The funnel is just a cylinder of foil and the mast is a cocktail stick. You can identify your own boats by painting the masts or funnels.

6 Finally, glue the cabins into place onto the hull. Your boat is now ready for launching! Put it carefully onto the water.

Each player has a fleet of boats and takes it in turns to flick tiddlywinks at the opposing fleet. Be careful not to hit your own boats. Last one afloat is the winner. The boat floats even though there are holes in it because the water has a sort of invisible 'skin'. It's an effect called 'surface tension.' However, if you knock the boat, the skin breaks – and the boat sinks.

You'll need:

sticky tape

a sponge

a drinking straw

a lolly stick

a kebab skewer

thick cardboard

a crisp tube (like a Pringles® container)

2 thick rubber bands

cardboard tube from a roll of foil

a sweet tube

a plastic tray

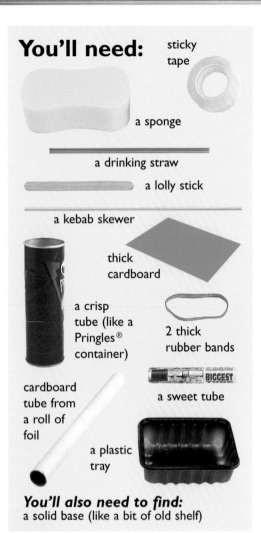

You'll also need to find:
a solid base (like a bit of old shelf)

The Hammer Hand of Horror Game

This is a great fun game for two players. You take it in turns to steal sweets, until suddenly the horrid hammer whacks you!

1 The base of the hammer mechanism is a cut-down crisp tube. Cut slots on opposite sides, and tape them down inside the tube. The slots should be slightly wider than the tube from the roll of foil. Now make two holes, one on either side of the crisp tube, as shown.

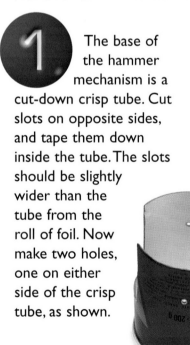

2 To construct the hammer arm, start by making two holes in the cardboard tube. The holes should be about 2cm from one end. Push a short piece of drinking straw through the two holes. Cut a small notch at the same end of the tube, as in the picture.

3 Attach the hammer arm to the base by pushing a length of kebab skewer through one of the holes in the crisp tube, then through the straw in the hammer arm, and then out through the other side of the tube. Trim off the ends and fix the skewer in place with two blobs of glue. This is a good time to decorate your arm...

Cut two rubber bands to make two lengths of rubber. Tape one end of each piece of rubber to the hammer arm. With the arm upright, tape each of the other ends to the side of the crisp tube so that the bands run over the notch in the tube. Now, when you lower the arm, it will tighten the rubber, making a spring mechanism.

Now cut out a square of thick cardboard, and glue the entire hammer mechanism to it.

6 Make a hole in a sponge and stick it on the top of the hammer arm to make the head of the hammer. Push a lolly stick into the outside of the sponge and glue it in place.

Now the whole mechanism is complete, glue it down firmly to a piece of wood (a length of old shelving is ideal!).

8 The secret sweet store is just a plastic tray. Glue a sweet tube underneath the tray, so it can rock back and forward.

9. Then set up the mechanism and tray so that the lolly stick rests under the lip of the tray, and the weight of the sweets holds the hammer in place. The idea is that as you remove sweets, the tray gets lighter and lighter until – BANG – it can't hold the hammer down any more.

10. The players sit either side and take it in turns to put their hands in the danger zone – just where they'll get whacked with the hammer – and remove one sweet at a time. The person who gets hit first has to give all their sweets to the other player!

Another version of the game is called the Grabbing Gorilla. Instead of the sponge hammer head, it uses a rubber gorilla hand from a joke shop and the base is covered in paper leaves.

Boat in a Bottle

Send a model boat crashing through a stormy sea...

You'll need:

food colouring

oil (baby or vegetable)

4 lolly sticks

You'll also need to find:
water, sand paper, 4 drawing pins, a small piece of matchstick

a clear plastic bottle

1 You can use any clear plastic bottle – an old mineral water one works well. Take off the label, and half fill the bottle with oil. Baby oil is best, as it's clear and smells nice – but you can use vegetable oil if that's all you've got.

2 Next, make up some coloured water in a jug. Any colour will work – but blue looks very nice. Add the coloured water to the bottle, so that it's almost full. Water is denser than oil, so it sinks to the bottom. When you rock the bottle, the oil and water stay separate – and you get lovely slow sloshy waves!

3 The finishing touch is to add a little boat made from four lolly sticks. First cut all the lolly sticks in half and glue four halves together in a pile. Use a bit of sand paper to shape the front of your boat into a point.

4 To get the weight just right so it floats nicely, stick four drawing pins in the bottom. And to make it look even more like a boat, add a bit of lolly stick as a cabin and a piece of matchstick as a funnel.

5 Pop the boat into the bottle, put the lid on tight and prepare to ride the waves!

Explosive Rockets

You'll need:

a little bit of toilet paper

bicarbonate of soda

lemon juice

a 35mm film container (the translucent ones work best)

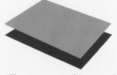
sticky tape

stiff paper or thin card

a small crisp tube (or a long one cut to size)

These rockets are very easy to make, and will fly pretty high!

1 Take the lid off the film container. Cut a strip of paper or thin card about 20cm long, roll it around the container and glue it along the edge to make a cylinder. This is the body of the rocket. The film container should be able to fit in at the bottom, with the open end downwards.

2 To make the top of the rocket – the 'nose cone' – cut a paper circle, and cut out a wedge. Then stick the edges together to make a cone shape and stick it to the top of the cylinder.

3 You can decorate your rocket with silver foil or tape to make it look more space age. If you want to, you can stick on some paper fins, but make sure you leave the very bottom of the rocket clear, so that you can still push in the film container.

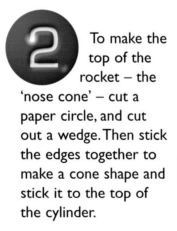

Finally, make a launch pad out of a small crisp tube turned upside down.

Now we're nearly ready for launch. Pour lemon juice into the film container until it's about half full. Then clamp on the lid with the package attached.

At this point, the two halves of the rocket fuel aren't mixed, so it's safe to carry it to the launch pad. But keep it pointed away from your face, just in case.

SAFETY FIRST

Some very important safety points. NEVER stand directly over the rocket when it's loaded; and if it doesn't go off, leave it a long, long time before you go back to it – just in case!

And only launch outdoors, because the rocket will leave a mess on the ground.

Now make the rocket fuel! It comes in two halves that explode when mixed, so be careful.

5 Cut out a 6cm disc from a single sheet of toilet paper. Put about half a teaspoonful of bicarbonate of soda on the middle, and twist the paper up into a neat package. Then tape the package to the inside of the lid of the film container, so it will hang down.

8 At the launch pad, turn the cardboard rocket upside down. Push the film container into the bottom of the rocket, keeping the container upright.

9 Then turn the rocket the right way up, place it on the launch pad and STAND CLEAR! The lemon juice will soak through the toilet paper, and mix with the bicarbonate of soda, creating a gas called carbon dioxide. Once the gas pressure has built up, the lid will suddenly pop off, and the rocket section will be blasted upwards into space…

Air-powered Racing Cars

These air-powered cars can go really fast, and are great fun to race.

You'll need:

4 bottle tops

a small mineral water bottle

a drinking straw

2 kebab skewers

First make your car...

1 The wheels for your car are bottle tops. Get some help to make holes in the centre of four bottle tops.

2 To make the axles for the wheels, cut two kebab skewers so that they are 2cm longer than the width of the bottle. Then cut two straws so they're a little bit shorter.

3 For each kebab skewer in turn, put a bottle top on one end, push the skewer through the straw, and attach another bottle top at the other end. A blob of glue will hold the wheels (bottle tops) firmly to the axles (kebab skewers).

4 Now glue the straws to the mineral water bottle, as shown. Make sure the axles can rotate freely inside the straws, and that the wheels don't wobble too much.

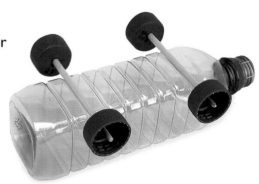

Now to create the engines! First, here's how to make a jet propelled car...

You'll need:

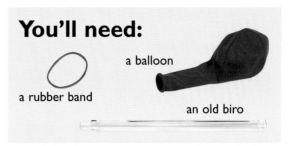

a rubber band

a balloon

an old biro

Dismantle the biro to leave just the plastic barrel. Make holes in the top and rear of the car (the side and bottom of the bottle), so you can slide the pen barrel through it. The pen barrel nozzle should point backwards.

6 Push the balloon on to the blunt end of the biro barrel, and secure it tightly with a rubber band.

To 'fuel' your car, just blow up the balloon through the pen barrel and then cover the nozzle with your thumb. When you put the car on the floor and uncover the nozzle, the air from the balloon is forced out through the nozzle and it pushes the car forward.

A large nozzle will give you lots of thrust, so the car will go fast – but the fuel will run out quickly. A smaller nozzle will give less thrust, but for much longer.

You don't have to use jet power though. Here's how to make a propeller engine...

You'll need:

rubber band

a piece of card

a paper clip

2 bottle tops

2 lolly sticks

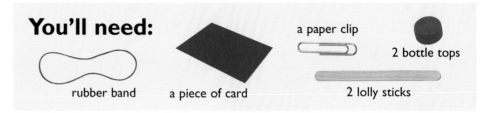

8 Get some help to cut two slits in one of the bottle tops, on opposite sides and at an angle. Now cover the open end of the bottle top with a disc made of cardboard, with cuts in it that line up with the top of the slits.

bottle tops

paper clip

cardboard washer

cardboard disc

9 Straighten out a paper clip and thread it through the centre of the bottle top and cardboard disc. Bend the end over and glue it in place on the cardboard.

10 Next put a little cardboard disc on the paper clip – a kind of washer. Rub the disc on both sides with a pencil, which will lubricate it and help it to spin freely.

11 Put another bottle top onto the paper clip, as shown. Bend the end of the paper clip into a hook.

12 Now make the propeller blades. These are just bits of cardboard cut to shape. Slide them into the slits in the bottle top. You have now completed the propeller assembly.

13 Glue a couple of lolly sticks to the back of the car in an upside down V shape. Now glue the propeller assembly in place, as shown.

14 The fuel for this engine is a large rubber band. Attach it to the paper clip hook, then stretch the other end over the front of the car (the neck of the bottle).

Wind the propeller up to get the car ready to race. But be careful not to over-wind, or break the engine!

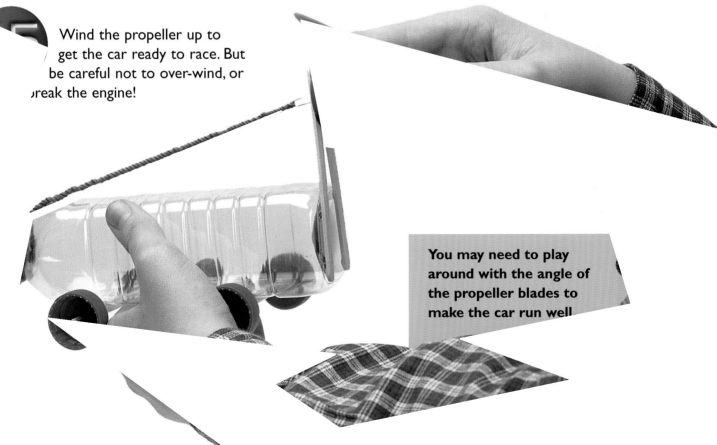

You may need to play around with the angle of the propeller blades to make the car run well

Pinball Wizard

This is a really groovy project – a pinball machine, complete with flippers and bells!

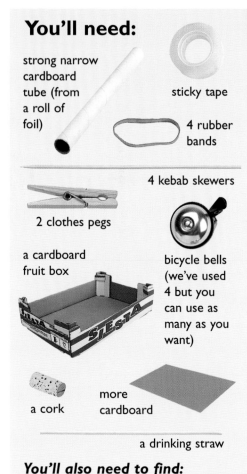

1 Prepare the base of the pinball machine by cutting the raised corners off a fruit box, to leave a level edge all round. Now cut a piece of card, so it's the same size as the inside base of the box. (This needs to have a very smooth surface, so the marbles can roll on it freely.)

2 Make some marble-sized holes in the smooth card (for traps) and stick it in position. Then make some small holes in the base where you want obstacles. Cut some 4cm lengths of kebab skewer, and glue them into place.

3 Next cut a strip of card, about 10cm longer than the width of the box, and about 5cm wide. Stick this in place at one end of the box, to make a curved boundary for the marbles to bounce off.

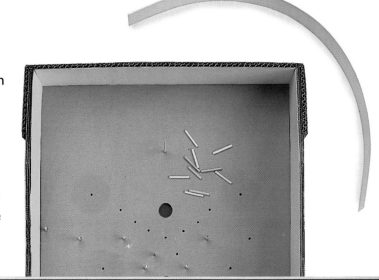

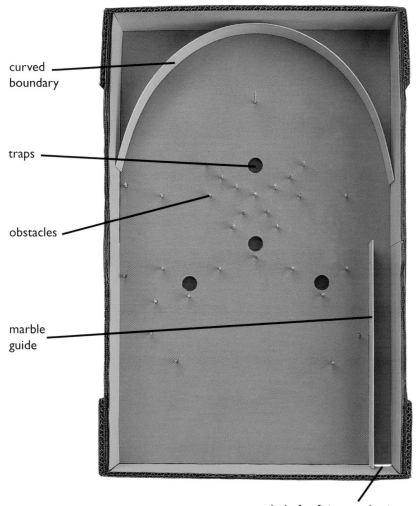

curved
boundary

traps

obstacles

marble
guide

hole for firing mechanism

4 At the other end of the box, cut a hole for the mechanism that will fire the marbles. The hole should be close to one of the long edges, slightly larger than the cardboard tube. Also glue a marble guide in place – it's just a length of card, as in the picture.

5 Now make the firing mechanism. First take the cork and a kebab skewer. Cut a piece of kebab skewer to about 3cm longer than the width of the top of the cork. Glue the piece of kebab skewer across the top of the cork. Jam a bead on either end to make it easy to hold, and carefully push the cork into the cardboard tube until the skewer handle stops it going any further.

Tape two rubber bands to either side of the cardboard tube. Loop the bands over the kebab skewer handle so that when you pull the cork out, the bands stretch and when you let go, the cork flies back into the tube.

7 Now push the cardboard tube through the hole in the base, and glue it in place inside so that the firing mechanism is outside the box.

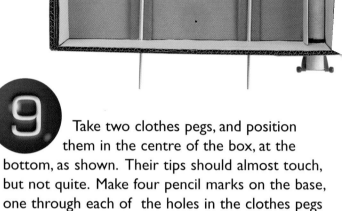

And here's how to make the flippers!

8 First cut two lengths of plastic straw (about 6cm) and glue them on to two pieces of cardboard for support. These are the guides for the kebab skewer controllers that will push the flippers. Make two holes in the edge of the box (for the kebab skewers to pass through); line up the straws and glue the guides in place.

9 Take two clothes pegs, and position them in the centre of the box, at the bottom, as shown. Their tips should almost touch, but not quite. Make four pencil marks on the base, one through each of the holes in the clothes pegs and the others in a diagonal just above the pegs. (These marks show the position of the supports for the flippers.)

10 The supports are made from bits of kebab skewer a little taller than the height of the pegs when they are lying in flipper position. Make holes in the base of the box on the pencil marks, and carefully push the bits of kebab skewer through, sticking them in place with glue.

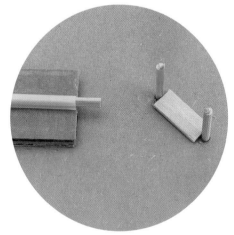

11 Wrap a rubber band around each clothes peg and position the the pegs on the supports. Follow the picture to get the rubber bands in the right place – they have to go round the supports in just the right way.

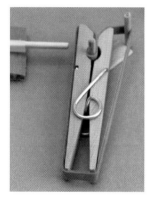

12 The flippers are opened and closed using kebab skewer controllers, pushed through the drinking straw guides. They should be long enough so that when they're operating the flippers, there's about 8cm outside the box for you to hold...

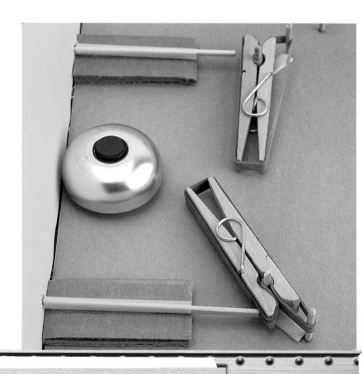

You can make the game exciting by making obstacles and obstructions for the marbles to bounce off. You can make bouncy barriers by looping more rubber bands over the kebab skewer obstacles. The spinner is made from two bits of card glued to a length of straw, and mounted on a piece of kebab skewer.

Finally, decorate your pinball table to make it look snazzy – and start practising to become a pinball wizard!

14 To score, use bicycle bells mounted on more bits of kebab skewer. Every time the marble rings a bell, you get a point!

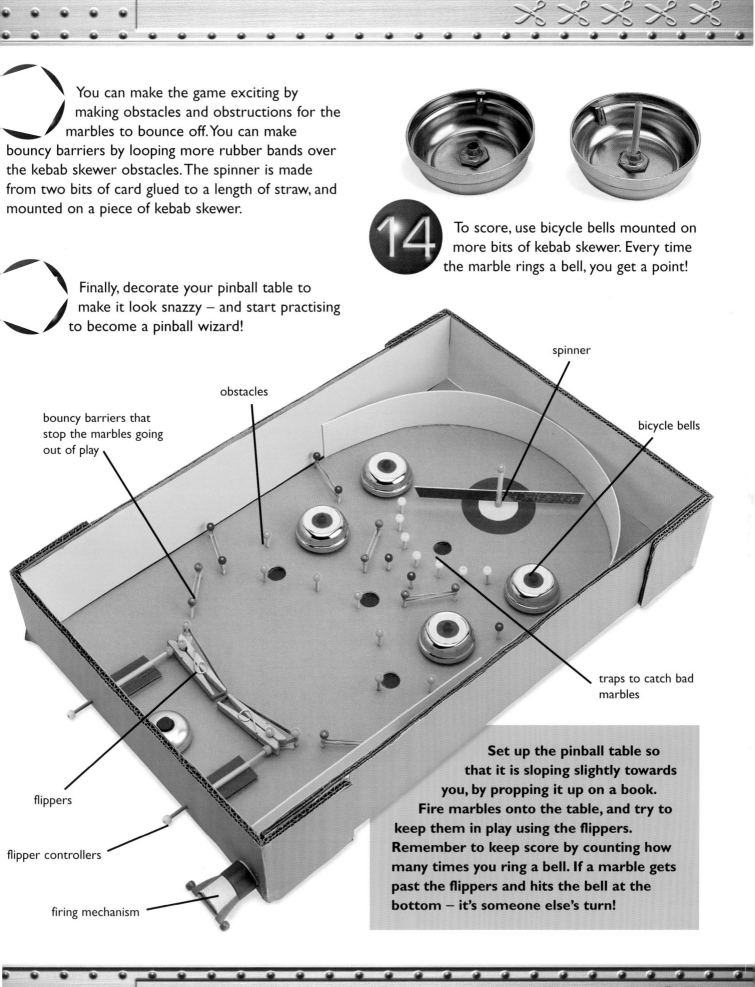

spinner

bicycle bells

obstacles

bouncy barriers that stop the marbles going out of play

traps to catch bad marbles

flippers

flipper controllers

firing mechanism

Set up the pinball table so that it is sloping slightly towards you, by propping it up on a book. Fire marbles onto the table, and try to keep them in play using the flippers. Remember to keep score by counting how many times you ring a bell. If a marble gets past the flippers and hits the bell at the bottom – it's someone else's turn!

CD Dragster

Here's something exciting to do with those junk CDs. It's a drag-tastic flywheel powered dragster...

You'll need:

- some bits of stiff card
- double sided sticky tape
- some thin, strong string
- 2 lolly sticks
- a kebab skewer
- 5 plastic cotton reels
- 4 CDs
- a wire coat-hanger
- strong sticky tape
- a piece of thin garden cane
- a drinking straw
- a milkshake straw (like a drinking straw but thicker!)
- narrow cardboard tube (like you get inside cling film rolls)
- 2 paper clips
- 2 plastic bottle tops

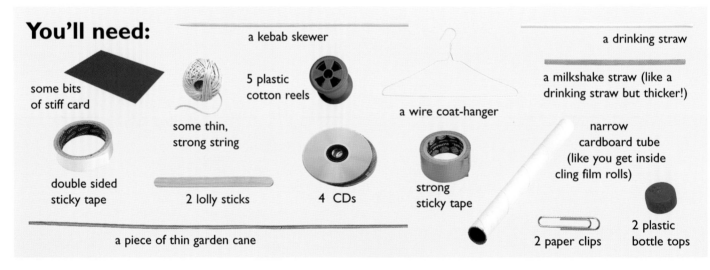

1 First make the back wheels. Take the four CDs, and stick them together into two pairs, with double sided sticky tape. Then glue a plastic cotton reel to each pair – and it's VITAL that they're slap bang in the centre, so do this CAREFULLY.

2 Now glue another cotton reel in between the ones that are glued to the CDs. Again do it carefully, and make sure that the milkshake straw can pass easily through the centre holes. This is now the wheel assembly.

3 Now make the axle. This is just the milkshake straw reinforced with a length of thin garden cane going through it. The axle should be as long as the wheel assembly, plus two cotton reels. Push this into position.

Now for the hubcaps. First take two more cotton reels and cut out four circles of stiff card, the same size as the ends. Two of these are going to be washers to allow the wheels to spin more freely. These two need milkshake straw sized holes in the centre so that the axle will fit.

5 The other two circles of card are the end caps for the cotton reels. Make two small holes in each, on either side of the centre, to match the 'outside' holes in the end of the cotton reel and glue them on.

Almost there! Take the wheel assembly and slide the washers on to each end of the axle. Now push on the cotton reels with the card tops. Finally, make two U shapes from short lengths of paper clip, and push them loosely into the two small holes.

7 Now for the body of the dragster. This starts as a narrow cardboard tube and a wire coat-hanger. Get someone who's good with pliers to clip off the hook and the bottom bar of the coat-hanger and bend it to shape, as shown. The distance between the legs needs to be exactly the same as the full width of the wheel assembly.

8. Now use strong sticky tape to attach the coat-hanger to the cardboard tube, so that the legs extend slightly beyond the end of the tube. To strengthen the body, jam and glue a lolly stick near the join. And finally, add some dragster decoration!

9. Next, make the front wheels. Glue a length of drinking straw on to a lolly stick, and pass a kebab skewer through the straw. Cut it so that it extends about 1cm on either side. Now take two plastic bottle tops and make small holes in the centre, so you can push them on the end of the kebab skewer. You don't need to glue these.

10. Now attach the body to the back wheels. Pass the tips of the coat-hanger legs through the loops of paperclip wire, and use a dab of glue to hold them in position.

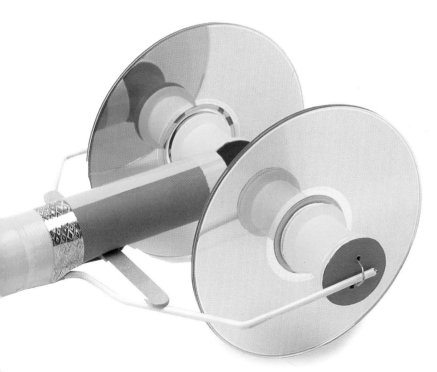

11. Next, glue the front wheel assembly underneath the front of the tube – making sure that the wheels are straight and level.

12 And that's the dragster finished! Now to add the power... a piece of thin, strong string. Wind it round the central cotton reel at the back – and make sure you wind it the right way so the dragster goes forwards, not backwards!

To race your dragster pull the string firmly, put the dragster down, and watch it go!

Beautiful Bouncing Birds

These flapping friends
will fly gracefully above your head...

You'll need:

4 rubber bands

string

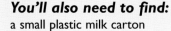
length of garden cane

a large
sheet of white
card and brown paper

6 twopence pieces
(for ballast!)

You'll also need to find:
a small plastic milk carton

1. Barn owls are brown on top and white underneath. So first, stick some brown paper onto a sheet of white card. Then mark out shapes for the wings, and cut them out.

2. Make four holes on each wing – two at the edge, and two about a third of the way into the wing, as in the picture. It's very important the holes match on both wings. Thread rubber bands through the holes nearest the inside edges of the wings, and secure them by passing the top loop through the bottom loop.

3. Next, take six twopence pieces, and glue three on each wing, just in from the outside edge. When the glue is set, cover them with a small piece of brown paper.

4. Wash out a plastic milk carton, then connect the wings by putting the elastic bands around it. Line up the wings so they are on diagonally opposite sides of the carton.

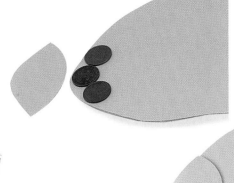

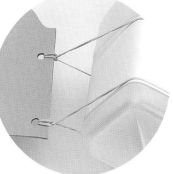

5 Next, make your creation look more like a bird by covering the top of the milk carton with brown paper, and the bottom with white card. Then cut out shapes for the face and tail and stick them on (but make sure you leave the end of the carton open so that you can adjust the balance later). Add some eyes and a beak.

7 At this stage the owl won't look very realistic, because the balance isn't right. To correct it, simply turn the bird face down, and pour some water into the milk carton. Add a bit at a time until the bird hangs and flies correctly… And putting a slight bend in each wing helps, too.

6 Now to make your bird fly! Take two equal lengths of string, and thread them through the holes in the middle of the wings. Attach the loose ends to a piece of stick.

8 The bird flaps its wings because it's like a pendulum – there's a pivot at the top and a swinging weight at the bottom. In fact, it's a series of pendulums connected together.

You don't have to make an owl... Using different sized containers, you can create a whole aviary of different birds – like this duck made from a squeezy ketchup bottle!

Musical Makes

2

Pig-a-phone

This little piggy goes 'oink oink oink' all the way home.

You'll need:

a cardboard tube, the wider the better

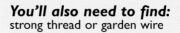

a straw, pink if possible

a balloon, preferably pink

You'll also need to find:
strong thread or garden wire

1 Cut the mouthpiece off the balloon. Put a blob of glue on the tip of the straw and stick it to the inside centre of the balloon. Tie the balloon over the straw as well, using the strong thread or garden wire.

2 Now turn the balloon inside out, and stretch it over the end of the tube.

3 Tape the balloon to the tube – and that's the instrument made! You play it by moistening your fingers, and pulling them along the straw. With a bit of practice, you'll be able to make the piggy oink!

head pattern

glue flap

slit

leg pattern

glue flap

4 To make your pig-a-phone look more like a pig, cover the tube in pink card. Then you can use these shapes as patterns to make the head and four legs – scale them up to the size you need, cut them out, bend them around, and glue them in place.

The tighter the skin of the balloon, the more high pitched the piggy's oink!

Roaring Rain Sticks

You'll need:

a hole punch

4 drinking straws

9 plastic drinking cups

some card

sticky tape

silver balls used for decorating cakes (or something else to make the sound of the rain)

Traditional Rain Sticks come from South America and make the sound of heavy rain falling. They're used to summon rain in the dry season. This one sounds just as good...

1 Cut the bottoms out of seven cups and keep two cups intact. Cutting plastic is pretty hard, so you may need some help. (Nine cups is a good number to give a long rain sound, but you can use any amount.)

2 Arrange your cups into pairs. One pair should have an intact cup, because it will be the bottom of the rain stick. You should have one intact cup left over.

3 Next cut out five cardboard circles for each pair of cups – two circles should be the same size as the bottom of the cup, two the same size as the middle, and one the same size as the top. If you're using eight cups, you should end up with eight small circles, eight middle-sized circles, and four large circles. Punch a hole in the centre of each circle.

4 Now punch more holes in the circles of card, and snip out small bits around the edges. The silver balls will fall through these gaps to make the rain sound...

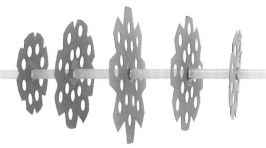

5. Next stick the circles of card on to drinking straws. Use one straw for each pair of cups, and arrange the small circles at either end of the straw and the bigger ones in the middle, as shown.

6. Now construct your rain stick. Place two cups over each straw, and tape them together. Then tape your four cup-pairs together. Remember to make sure that the bottom cup in your rain stick is the one that really does have a bottom, otherwise all the silver balls will go straight through!

7. Pour the silver balls in at the top, and then seal your rain stick by putting the remaining cup over the open end and taping it in place.

8. Now you're ready to make it rain. Just turn the stick upside down, and all the silver balls will pour from one end to the other...

If you haven't got any silver balls, you can use anything that's small enough to fall through the holes. Dried lentils work quite well!

Zany Zithers

You'll need:

4 poster tubes with plastic ends

4 small and 4 large rubber bands

4 clothes pegs

a large cardboard box

These musical instruments have a very sweet sound – and are dead easy to make and play!

1 Start by cutting a rubber band so that you can stretch it out.

2 Attach one end of the rubber band to one end of a poster tube, by jamming it in with the tube's plastic cap.

3 Stretch the rubber band the length of the tube, and secure the other end the same way as before – by jamming it with the plastic end cap.

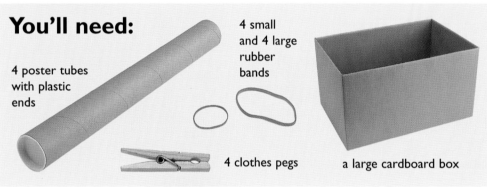

4 Now wedge a clothes peg under the rubber band, and stand it on the tube. Bind the legs of the peg together with another rubber band. You'll need to make four of these all together.

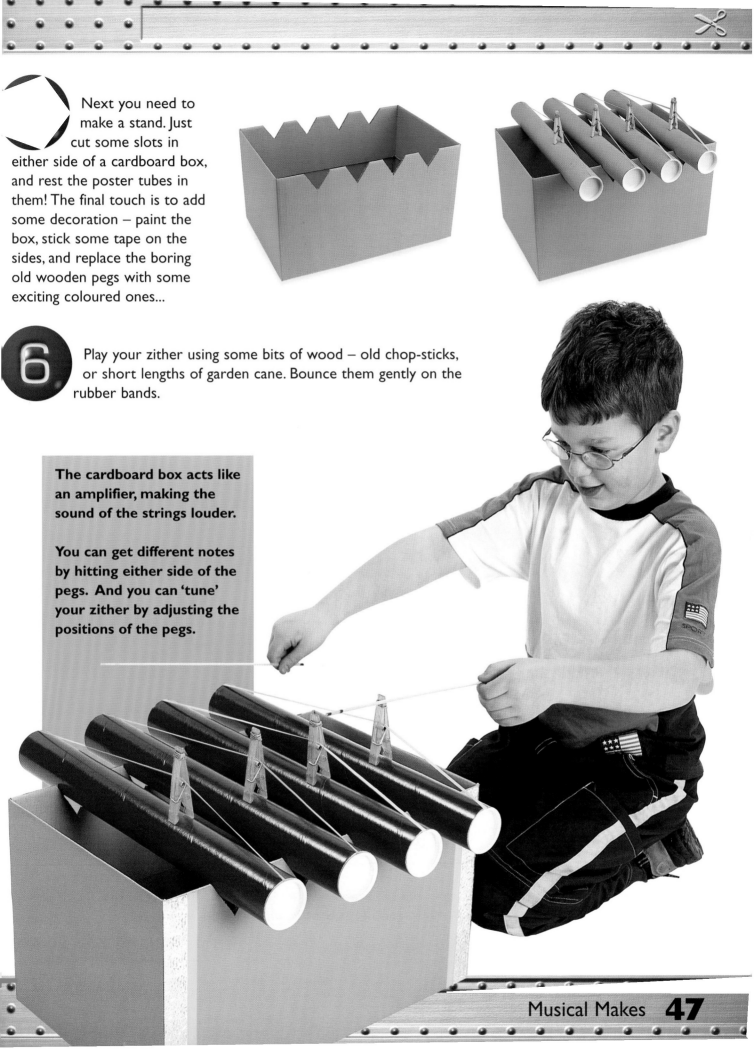

Next you need to make a stand. Just cut some slots in either side of a cardboard box, and rest the poster tubes in them! The final touch is to add some decoration – paint the box, stick some tape on the sides, and replace the boring old wooden pegs with some exciting coloured ones...

6. Play your zither using some bits of wood – old chop-sticks, or short lengths of garden cane. Bounce them gently on the rubber bands.

The cardboard box acts like an amplifier, making the sound of the strings louder.

You can get different notes by hitting either side of the pegs. And you can 'tune' your zither by adjusting the positions of the pegs.

Droning Dragon-o-phones

These delightful dragons can make magnificent music!

You'll need:

- a balloon
- sticky tape
- a cereal packet
- an old biro
- 2 ping-pong balls
- Blu-tack
- a poster tube
- a yoghurt pot (empty!)

1 Make a hole in the poster tube, about the size of a five-pence piece, and about half way up. Paint the tube a nice dragon-y colour (red, of course!).

2 Cut a hole in the base of the yoghurt pot, just the right size to take the poster tube. And make another hole in the side of the pot, just the right size to take the barrel of the old biro.

3 Cut the neck off a balloon, and stretch the rest of it over the top of the pot. (This isn't easy, because plastic yoghurt pots tend to crack, so you might need some help.) Tape the balloon securely to the pot.

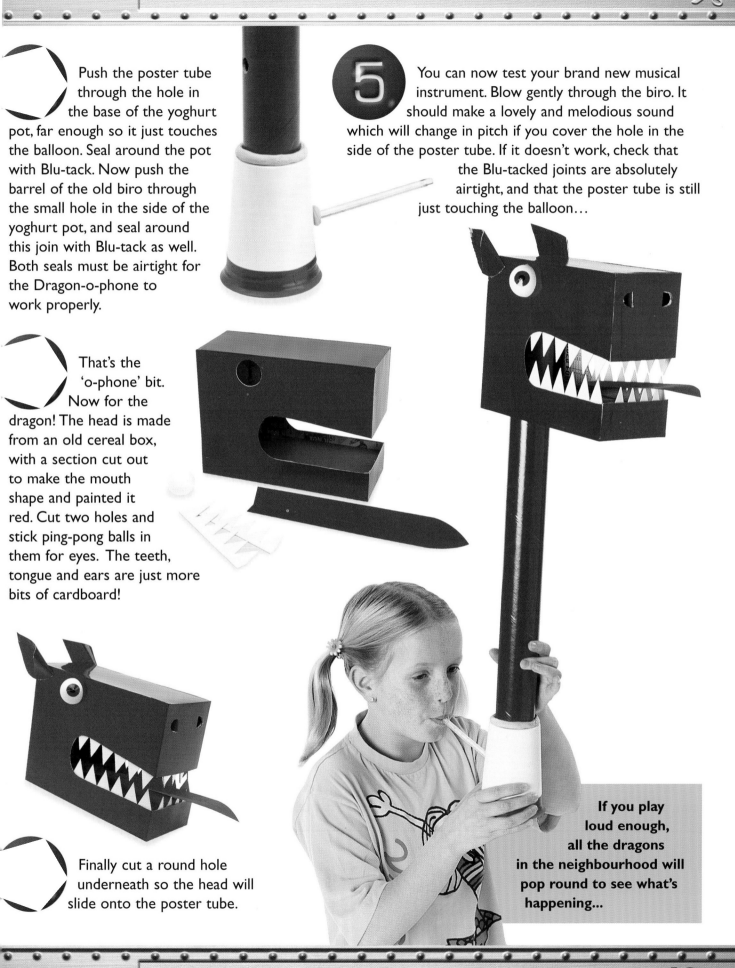

Push the poster tube through the hole in the base of the yoghurt pot, far enough so it just touches the balloon. Seal around the pot with Blu-tack. Now push the barrel of the old biro through the small hole in the side of the yoghurt pot, and seal around this join with Blu-tack as well. Both seals must be airtight for the Dragon-o-phone to work properly.

That's the 'o-phone' bit. Now for the dragon! The head is made from an old cereal box, with a section cut out to make the mouth shape and painted it red. Cut two holes and stick ping-pong balls in them for eyes. The teeth, tongue and ears are just more bits of cardboard!

Finally cut a round hole underneath so the head will slide onto the poster tube.

5 You can now test your brand new musical instrument. Blow gently through the biro. It should make a lovely and melodious sound which will change in pitch if you cover the hole in the side of the poster tube. If it doesn't work, check that the Blu-tacked joints are absolutely airtight, and that the poster tube is still just touching the balloon…

If you play loud enough, all the dragons in the neighbourhood will pop round to see what's happening…

Beat Box

This rhythm generator works in a similar way to a music box!

You'll need:

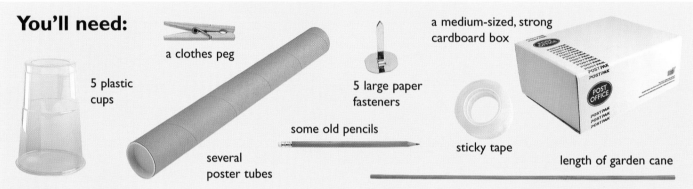

- a clothes peg
- 5 plastic cups
- several poster tubes
- 5 large paper fasteners
- some old pencils
- a medium-sized, strong cardboard box
- sticky tape
- length of garden cane

1 Make the sounding tubes. The length of these determines the pitch of the sound. Get someone to help you cut the poster tubes accurately to these lengths:

Tube 1: 48cm	Tube 2: 34cm
Tube 3: 26cm	Tube 4: 18cm
Tube 5: 14cm	

2 Now take five plastic cups and glue a large paper fastener to the bottom of each one. Then cut the bottom of the cups off, leaving about a centimetre of the sides attached. Throw away the sides – they're not needed.

3 The bases will then fit neatly over the ends of the poster tubes. Tape them in place.

4 Now arrange the sounding tubes in length order, and glue them to a piece of stiff card that's roughly the same width as your cardboard box. The most important thing is that the ends are exactly level with each other, so the paper fasteners are all lined up, and all flat.

Tape up the cardboard box so it's completely sealed. Cut a flap at one end (see the picture for where to make the cuts). Fold the flap underneath to strengthen the top of the box. This is important, because the support must be rigid for the mechanism to work.

Now lay the sounding tube array on top of the box, and make a mark on the vertical halves of poster tubes at the same level as the fasteners. Then cut a slot in both vertical half-tubes, down to that level, and wide enough to take the garden cane.

Assemble the tube with the two end caps, and the cane, and glue it all together. And finally, glue a clothes peg to the long protruding bit of cane, as a handle.

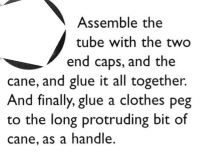

6 Get another length of poster tube that's about 6cm higher than the box. Cut it in half lengthways and stick the two halves on opposite sides of the slot (as shown).

8 Measure the distance between the two half-tubes, and cut another poster tube to just slightly less than that length, so it fits in between. This will be the musical barrel. Take two poster tube end caps, and make a hole in the centre of them, so that you can pass the piece of garden cane all the way through. Cut the garden cane so it's a bit longer than the tube at one end, and about 6cm longer at the other.

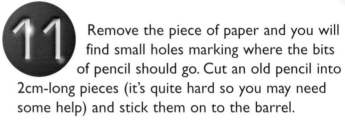

10 Almost there… The last step is to program the musical barrel to play a tune! This is a bit hit and miss, but the principle is that you attach bits of pencil to the barrel in the right places so that as you turn the handle, they 'pluck' the paper fasteners. One way to find the right places, is to get a piece of paper that will fold exactly around the barrel, and rule out eight lines on it. Stick it lightly on to the barrel, and decide which note you want played on each line. Punch through where the line and the paper fastener touch as you turn the handle. (To help you plan your tune – the longer the tube is, the deeper the note will be…)

11 Remove the piece of paper and you will find small holes marking where the bits of pencil should go. Cut an old pencil into 2cm-long pieces (it's quite hard so you may need some help) and stick them on to the barrel.

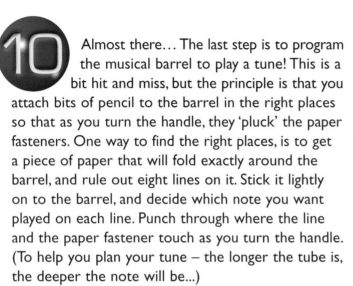

If you get bored with this rhythm, you can simply create more barrels with differen tunes on them!

12 Place the barrel in the supports, and hold it in place with a rubber band at each end, and then you're almost ready to play! The very last thing to do, is to get the sounding tube array in exactly the right place. The ends of the paper fasteners should just be flicked by the bits of pencil – too close, and it'll jam; too far away, and it won't play at all! Once you've got it in the right position, hold it down firmly, and off you go. Turn the barrel gently by using just your finger to push the peg around.

Bongo Boo Bams

This is a great percussion instrument!

You'll need:

sticky tape

some old tin cans

a can opener

1 First wash and dry each can, and remove the labels – they should come off easily in hot soapy water.

2 Then remove the bottom of some cans. Make sure you use a can opener that leaves smooth edges. (Can openers can be quite tricky, so get someone to help you.) You'll need one can that still has its bottom for each bongo boo bam you want to make.

Now use the sticky tape to join the cans into a long column. You should be able to see right through the column.

Finally, add a normal can (one that still has its bottom) to one end of the column. And use some more tape to decorate your boo bams...

And that's it - the bongo boo bam is finished! To play it, just bang the closed end on the floor – it sounds good on carpets!

The note that's produced depends on the number of cans. The longer the column, the deeper the note. In fact, if you double the length, you go down an octave. Try this out by making bongo boo bams of different lengths.

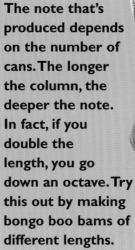

Arty Makes

Inspiring Spirals

These drinking straw mobiles are simple and pretty.

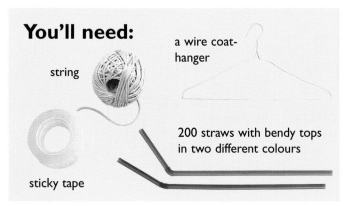

You'll need:

string

a wire coat-hanger

sticky tape

200 straws with bendy tops in two different colours

1. First organise your bendy straws. Take two at a time – one of each colour – and arrange them so the straight bits are together, with the bendy bits protruding at each end.

2. Tape the two straws together in the middle, then make a hole in the tape, right in the middle between the straws. Do this for all your straws. Then get someone to help you straighten out a wire coat-hanger and very carefully thread the pairs of straws on to the wire.

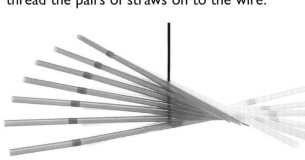

Fan the straws out as you go, so they look neat, and glue them in place. The very last thing is to attach a piece of string to the top of your mobile, so you can hang it up.

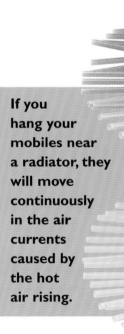

If you hang your mobiles near a radiator, they will move continuously in the air currents caused by the hot air rising.

These spiral mobiles make magnificent moving decorations...

You'll need:

a ping-pong ball

a large poster tube

string

coloured sticky tape

a kebab skewer

1 The simplest spiral mobiles start as poster tubes. Get some brightly coloured tape, and follow the spiral seam up the outside of the tube.

2 Then cut on both sides of the tape, following the spiral. This is quite hard, so you might need help from someone with strong hands...

3 Support the spiral by gluing a bit of kebab skewer across the top. Then tie a piece of string to the skewer, and it's ready to hang!

To make your simple mobile look really mind-boggling, glue a ping-pong ball in the middle of the spiral. As it turns, it looks just like the ball is moving up and down the spiral. Weird!

Harmonograph Masterpieces

This is an automatic art producing machine!

You'll need:

 string

 a seed tray

 3 lolly sticks

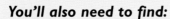 a straw

a clothes peg

a piece of thick card

a lump of Blu-tack

a kebab skewer

a knitting needle

You'll also need to find:
2 lengths of wood (things like mops or brooms)
2 chairs, some sand or a heavy object, a pile of
books, a felt-tip pen, a cardboard box and paper

1 First set up the two chairs and lengths of
wood, as shown in the picture.

2 Now put
something heavy in
the seed tray to weight it down. You
could use sand or books, or some other heavy
object.

3 Cut a piece of card
so it's just slightly
larger than the
rim of the seed tray.
You'll need to cut off the
corners of the card, so you can loop a
piece of string under each end of the tray.
Tape the string into place. Then tie the
ends of the string to the poles resting on the chairs, and
hang the tray so that it's level.

4 Now make
the pen arm.
Tape a clothes peg
to the end of a knitting
needle, and clip a felt-tip pen
in place.

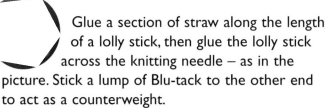

Glue a section of straw along the length of a lolly stick, then glue the lolly stick across the knitting needle – as in the picture. Stick a lump of Blu-tack to the other end to act as a counterweight.

Glue two lolly sticks inside a cardboard box so that they are as far apart as the length of your kebab skewer. Now slide the skewer inside the straw, and glue the skewer to the two lolly sticks. And that's the pen arm complete!

Set the pen arm as in the picture, using a pile of books to get it to the right height. Stick a piece of paper to the card and adjust the amount of Blu-tack on the end of the pen arm so the pen rests lightly in the middle of the paper.

Now lift the pen up and set the tray swinging. Gently lower the pen and beautiful works of art will automatically be produced.

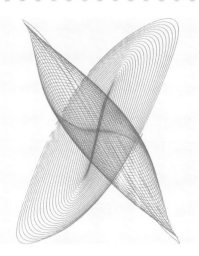
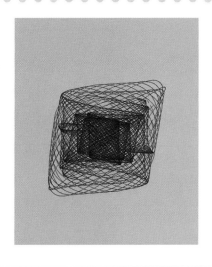
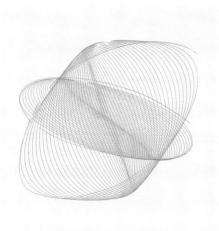

Two-way Pictures

These amazing pictures look like one photo from one part of the room, and a different photo from another!

1 Start with two photos or printed pictures that are the same size. You will be cutting them up, so make sure nobody will mind!

2 Draw pencil lines on the pictures, all the same width apart. For A4-sized pictures, make the lines about 2cm apart. For smaller photos, use closer lines.

3 Cut the pictures into strips, using the pencil lines as a guide. Make sure you keep the strips in the correct order.

4 To make the backing cut a piece of card so that it's the same height as your pictures, but twice as wide. Then draw pencil lines on it, the same width apart as the ones you drew on the pictures. Score the lines to make the card easy to fold and then fold it into a concertina shape.

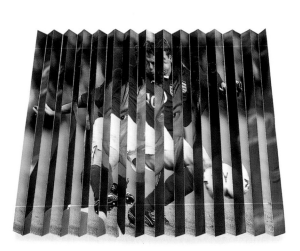

5 Now comes the fun bit! Glue the strips of the first picture on to the strips of card that face right and glue the strips of the second picture on to the strips of card that face left. Glue them accurately – and be very careful to keep them in the right order. And now you've got two pictures for the price of one!

Horrible Heads

...of the shrunken variety!

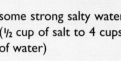

1 Start by peeling a large apple, leaving some skin at the top and bottom.

2 Now use the potato peeler to carve a face in the apple. Be careful, because potato peelers are VERY sharp – you might need to get someone to help you. Stick an opened-out paper clip in the top of the apple.

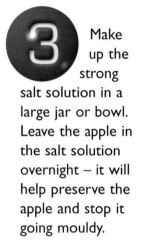

3 Make up the strong salt solution in a large jar or bowl. Leave the apple in the salt solution overnight – it will help preserve the apple and stop it going mouldy.

4 Let your shrunken head dry out for a couple of weeks. Put it somewhere warm and airy – near a radiator or on a windowsill.

5 When it's dry, gnarled and horrible, you've got the perfect prop to horrify your friends.

Try using matchsticks to make horrible-looking teeth. For hair use some wool, or the hair from an old doll. Use a drawing pin to hang some rotten-looking clothes from the bottom of the head.

CHAPTER FOUR

Teasing Tricks

Bouncing Corks

Can you drop a cork so it stands on its end? Every time? Here's how...

Most people drop the cork end on, which never works – the cork bounces all over the place.

1 The trick is to hold the cork sideways, about a cork and a half's height above the table. Let it go, and it'll bounce on to its end.

One and a half times the height of the cork.

2 If it doesn't work with a particular cork, just adjust the height slightly. It's the bounce that's crucial!

The Dreaded Coin, Stick and Glass Puzzle

Here's a puzzle to test your friends.

You'll need:

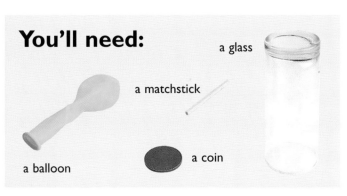

a glass

a matchstick

a coin

a balloon

1 Stand the coin on its side and balance the matchstick on it. Then cover the whole lot with a glass. The trick is to knock the match off the coin without touching the glass, the coin or the matchstick. Impossible? Not to Super Science Brain (that's you…).

2 When your friends have spent several hours puzzling and still can't do it, reveal the answer. It's done with the magic of static electricity!

3 Blow up the balloon and rub it against a woolly jumper to charge it up with static. Then move it close to the glass and – amazingly – the matchstick will jump off the coin!

It works because static electricity attracts everything towards it but only the matchstick is light enough to move.

The Tumbler Challenge

This trick's quite tricky – so you might need to practise it a bit before trying it on your mates.

You'll need:

2 tall plastic tumblers

a piece of card

And secretly:
a drinking straw

a jug of water

a deep tray

1 Fill both the tumblers with water, right to the brim. Place a piece of card on top of one of the tumblers.

2 Take the tumbler with the piece of card on it and carefully turn it upside down, holding the card in place. Put it on top of the other tumbler. Amazingly you will find that once the tumbler is upside down you can take your hand away from the card and it will stay in place.

3 Remove the card quickly, while holding the tumbler in place. Now challenge your mates to get the water out of the top tumbler without touching it… They won't be able to – but you can!

4 Here's how. Although it looks like the two tumblers are touching, in fact there are tiny gaps all round the rim – because the plastic is a bit bumpy. The water doesn't normally come out through these gaps because of its surface tension – it makes a sort of skin over the holes. But if you get a drinking straw and blow through it at the place where the two rims touch, the water will start to bubble out and the top tumbler will empty. It works because the extra force from the blowing breaks the surface tension – and then the water can squeeze out through the tiny gaps. And now you can see why you should do this trick on a deep tray…

Scary Book Bat

Put your mates off reading for life! This noisy, scary bat comes flapping out of a book when you open it...

Cut out a bat shape from the thick strong card. (The card needs to be strong enough to hold a stretched rubber band in position.) Make a hole in the centre of the bat shape, about half as big again as the keyring.

Stick the thin card bat shape to the thick card bat shape so that the holes line up, and the bat is hinged at its head. (You could add two little stickers for eyes.)

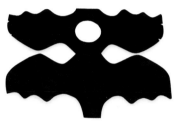

2 Use the bat shape as a template and cut a double bat shape from the thin black card, so the two shapes are connected at the bat's head. You only need the hole in one of the sides.

Now for the mechanism. Hitch two rubber bands to either side of the keyring, then make two little slots at the ends of the bat's wings. Stretch the bands across the bat and hook them into the little slots so that the keyring sits in the hole.

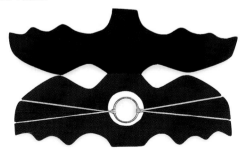

5 And here's how to scare your mate! Turn the keyring over and over to wind up the rubber bands – and wind up your friend! Fold down the bat-flap, and place it in the centre of a book. The hard bit is getting your mate to open the book without giving the game away!

Acknowledgements

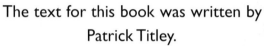

The text for this book was written by Patrick Titley.

The series producer of *The Big Bang* is Colin Nobbs. The ideas come from the production team, who are: Jonathan Sanderson, Richard Maude, Catherine White, Matthieu Barret, Nicola Hardy, Michelle Martin, Anna Perowne, Greg Taylor and Damien Wasylkiw. Many other people contribute to the success of the TV series, not least the amazing presenters, Gareth Jones and Violet Berlin.

Special thanks to Robyn Bullough, Anna Baker, Anthony Lojik, Daniel Lojik, Hannah Porter, William Rook, Joshua Rook and Rochelle Taylor, who appear in the photos.

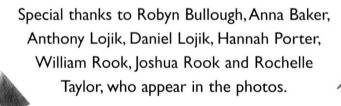